Giving and Taking

Fables on Where to Stop

Erin Yun

For those who have given,

and those who have taken.

Contents

These are simple stories.

They begin with familiar things—
effort, kindness, expectation.

They unfold as they are,
sometimes uneven,
sometimes unsettled.

They simply end.

A moment can be enough.

The Bird and the Nest

In spring,

a bird began building nests.

She had a gift for choosing branches—

which would bend just enough,

which would hold.

She could tell right away.

Before long,
other birds came to her.

She helped them.

Sometimes,
she added small touches—
a few pretty leaves,
little things
that made a nest feel complete.

More birds began to come.
They waited for her.

Some would bring branches,
just to have her look at them.

They liked
how her nests turned out.

Spring passed,
and still,
she had no nest of her own.

She kept building for others,
never stopping.

At last,
she began
to build for herself.

But by then,
it was already late spring.

She worked quickly—
branch after branch.

She didn't pause
to choose anymore.

Some branches didn't hold.
One slipped and fell.

The nest was small and shaky.
There wasn't much room.

When summer came,
her fledglings were finally born.

They were squished together,
restless and noisy,
pushing against each other.

Often, one or two
tumbled out of the nest.

Each day,
she patched the nest,
lifted fallen fledglings,
and searched for food.

No birds came to help.

The summer stretched on.

She was exhausted.

The next spring,
she started early.

This time,
she chose her branches
carefully.

She gathered more than enough.

A bird flew past.
"Could you take a look?"

She paused.

She did not go.

She set another branch
in place.

After that,
fewer birds came.

Then none.

She added berries
to her nest,
and a few flowers.

She took her time.

The nest held.

Her fledglings thrived.

The Turtle and the Road

A turtle moved slowly.

Along the road,
other animals would watch him.

They asked,
"Why are you so slow?"

He would stop,
take his time,
and answer carefully.

"My shell is heavy."
"I'm not slow–
I just move steadily."
"Each step has its place."

"Slow is calm."

Some nodded.
Some shook their heads.
Some didn't wait
and were already gone.

Each time he moved on,
he fell a little farther behind.

He had spent his time explaining.

Day after day,
he stopped to answer.

No one really listened.

One day,
as he made his way
down the road,
someone asked again—

"Why are you so slow?"

He paused,
looked ahead,
and kept moving.

He left the voice behind.

The road grew quiet.
He kept going.

And as he walked,
something began to change—

he didn't need to stop anymore.

His steps felt lighter.
He stopped explaining.

He drew his head into his shell,
then stretched it out again
and went on.

The road was long.

No one followed.

He was still slow—

but his journey was his own.

The Bee and the Flowers

Each day,
the bee flew far.

He carried pollen
from one place to another.

But the flowers always
had something to say.

"You're late."
"This doesn't smell right."
"The last one was better."

It was never enough.

The bee said nothing.

The next day,
he flew faster.

The day after that,
he went farther,
searching for something better.

Sometimes,
he chose places nearby,
just so
he could return sooner.

Still–

"This isn't right."
"It's not what we wanted."

The bee tried to explain.

The wind had been strong.
The blooms were different.
Some places were far.

The flowers were
not convinced.

"You've changed."

After that,
the bee stopped explaining.

For a while,
he still came.

Then one day, he didn't.

He landed instead
in another field.

There were many flowers there.

When he arrived,
one of them shifted slightly.

"You're here."

He set the pollen down.

No one asked
where he had been.

No one compared it
to what came before.

Nothing was corrected.
Nothing was measured.

The flowers welcomed him quietly.

The air was still.

The bee didn't have to rush.

He stayed.

The Bear and the Fox

In the forest,
there lived a bear
and a fox.

They were good friends.

One day,
a fallen tree pinned down
the bear's blanket.

He stood beside it,
pulling at it
but it wouldn't budge.

He saw the fox passing by
and called out,
"Could you help me move this?"

The fox stopped,
looked it over, and said,
"I'm busy."

Then he walked on.

The bear paused,
but said nothing.

He pulled at it himself—
slowly, for a long time.

At last,
he dragged it free.

It was wrinkled,
streaked with dirt.

He straightened it out
as best he could,
and kept it to himself.

A few days later,
a disturbance
spread through the forest.

Hunters had come.

Animals scattered.

The bear turned to leave,
but the path ahead was blocked.

He stopped.

Before he could think,
the fox appeared
from the side.

He shoved him
toward a narrow trail.

They ran.

After a while,
the sounds faded.

They slowed,
then stopped.

Neither of them spoke.

The bear stood there
for a while, thinking.

The path behind them was quiet.

And he never mentioned the tree again.

The Shop and the Lemons

A shop owner opened
a small lemonade shop.

At first, business was slow.

The lemons he used were
small and pale.

One day, a customer visited.

He had a tree at home—
large lemons, fragrant, unlike the rest.

He brought a few the next time.

The lemonade changed.

Customers noticed.

Soon, there was a line.

The man brought
more lemons.

Then more.

The shop grew.

New recipes appeared—
tarts, bread, cakes.

The owner worked hard.

He treated customers well.
He served them promptly.

But not the man.

He often stood in line
just to speak with the owner.

Over time,
the lemons were expected.

The deliveries, assumed.

The distance grew.

Still, the man came.

One day,

he never came again.

The Fox and the Rope

There was a fox in the forest.

One day,

he fell into a pit.

It wasn’t very deep,
but the sides were slick.

He jumped–
and slid back down.

He tried again.

He stopped.

After a while,
a deer passed by.

“Give me a hand,”
the fox called up.

The deer glanced down,
said nothing,
and walked on.

Later,
a group of monkeys came by,
playing by the pit.

“Find a vine,”
the fox called.
“Drop it down.”

They looked briefly,
didn’t move, and left.

The fox didn’t call out again.

He sat there
and waited.

No one came.

He looked up.

At the edge of the pit,
a short, broken vine hung down.

It was just out of reach.

He stood there for
a moment.

Then suddenly,
he jumped.

He missed.

He paused,
looked down
at where he stood.

It wasn't that low.

He stepped back
and jumped again.

This time,
his paw brushed the vine—
but he couldn't hold on.

He dropped back down.

After a while,

he turned
and started to run
along the bottom of the pit.

One circle.
Then another.
Faster each time.

He reached the edge—
and leapt.

This time,
he caught it.

He climbed out.

He stood above the pit
and looked back.

The vine
had always been there.

He had waited.
He had called.

But in the end,
no one threw a rope down.

He was the one

who started running.

The Squirrel and the Nuts

In autumn,
a squirrel gathered nuts.

Some were large.
Some were small.

He stored them
in different places.

Before long,
other animals came to him.

A rabbit asked,
"Could you spare some?"

The squirrel gave her
a few of the larger ones.

A small bird said,
"I only need a little."

The squirrel shared some.

A fox passed by,
glanced at the pile.

"These look good,"
he said.

The squirrel handed over
a few of the biggest ones—
the easiest to open.

Then, after a moment,
he added two more.

Days passed.

Each time he gave
something away,
he chose the better ones.

What remained
grew smaller.

When winter came,
he looked at his stockpile.

There were still nuts—
not many,
and all of them small.

The shells were hard.
He tried to crack one.

He paused.

It wouldn't open.

He picked another.

The squirrel sat there,
hungry for a long time.

He said nothing.

The next autumn,
he gathered again.

This time,
he set the largest ones aside
in a hidden place
and left them untouched.

The medium ones
he shared with passing animals.

Sometimes,
he gave a few larger ones—
but not all.

When winter came,
he opened the place
he had set aside.

The shells opened easily.

He had a warm,

well-fed winter.

The Pigs and the Basket

Three young pigs

had grown up

and gone their own ways.

Years passed.

One season,
they returned home,
each bringing food.

The first pig
set down a few fruits.

“I didn’t find much,”
he said.

“It’s good you came back,”
the parents said.

The second pig
set down a little more.

“I found some,” he said,
“but I ate most of it.”

“That’s alright,”
they said.
“You must have been hungry.”

The third pig
set down a full basket.

The fruit was fresh,
carefully chosen—
better than the rest.

“I gathered a lot,”
he said.
“But along the way,
there were others—
hungry,
so I gave much of it away.”

The parents looked into the basket.

Then looked at him.

"You had more," they said.

The third pig
did not answer.

"That
was not yours to give."

That night,
they ate what was brought back.

They took from his basket first.

No one spoke to him
for the rest of the night.

The next morning,
the basket sat
by the door.

He stood there for
a while.

Then he turned
and left.

The Fox and the River

In winter,
the river froze.

A young deer
stepped onto the ice.

It gave way.

The deer fell through
and struggled in the water.

A fox stood on the bank.

He watched for a while.

Then he stepped forward
and jumped in.

The water was bitterly cold.

He swam toward the deer,
circled behind it,
and caught hold of its fur.

Slowly,
he pulled it toward the shore.

The current pressed against them,
pulling them down.

He did not loosen his grip.

After a long while,
they reached the bank.

The deer was trembling.

The fox was trembling
too.

The fox stood still.
He said nothing.

He had only meant to help.

The deer looked at him—
at his teeth—
and stepped back.

"What were you doing?"

The fox did not answer.

After a while,
the deer ran into the forest.

In the days that followed,
rumors started.

"He pulls animals out of the water
because they're easier to eat on land."

"He waits until they're too weak to move,
then takes his time."

The fox heard.

He did not go after the deer.

He did not explain.

When spring came,
the ice began to break.

The river ran swift and cold.

One day,
the fox returned to the bank.

A goat had slipped.

Its front legs were in the water,
its body sliding downward.

The fox stopped
and hesitated.

The wind was strong.

After a while,
he turned away,
dragged over a huge fallen branch,
and set it by the water.

The goat caught hold of it
and pulled itself up.

The fox did not come closer.

He stood there,
then walked away.

The river kept flowing.

The Rabbit and the Fox

One winter,
a rabbit came upon a fox
lying in the snow.

The fox was thin, tired, and sick.

The rabbit brought the fox back
to her burrow.

After that,
she began going out each day
in search of food.

She looked for things
the fox would want—
berries, fish, kale—
things she herself would never eat.

Slowly,
the carrots in the burrow
disappeared.

At times, she would sit
and watch
as the fox ate.

She could not quite say
when this had become her role,
or why she remained in it.

She stopped wandering.
Stopped playing.

Her days grew smaller,
until they were shaped by
a single, quiet question:

what to bring back next.

Then one day,
the fox was gone.

No word.
No good-bye.

The burrow remained—
only emptier than before.

The rabbit stood there
for a long while.

She did not know
how to respond.

At last—

she stepped outside,
pulled a carrot
from the frozen soil,

and took a bite.

She paused.

It had been so long
since she had tasted one that
it felt almost unfamiliar—

and then,
suddenly, it did not.

She took another bite.

And then, quietly,
she began to laugh.

"I had this all along,"
she thought.

In the days that followed,
she gathered carrots again.

The burrow filled, slowly,
with what had been there before.

Another year went by.

Winter came again.

One evening,
on her way home,
she saw another animal
in the snow—

hungry
and almost motionless.

The rabbit hesitated.

Then she stepped forward,
placed two carrots beside it,
and withdrew.

She did not stay.

She did not bring it home.

Back in her burrow,
she finished her carrots
quietly.

And that night,
she slept—

deeply,
without interruption.

The Owl and the Squirrel

They lived in the same tree—
an owl and a squirrel.

Their lives rarely overlapped.

One belonged to the night.
The other to the day.

One evening,
they began to talk.

"The night is better,"
said the owl.
"It's quieter.
You notice more."

"The day is easier,"
said the squirrel.
"You can see where you're going.
You find what you need."

Neither was convinced.

They went back and forth
until there was nothing
left to say.

So they decided to try.

That night,
the squirrel stepped out
instead of staying in.

The forest felt unfamiliar.

Shapes shifted.
Paths seemed to disappear.

He wandered for
a long time
and found very little.

Once he nearly ran
straight into a tree.

Even the places he knew felt
strange to him.

The next morning,
the owl went out instead.

The light was too sharp.

He blinked,
moved slowly,
and kept missing his landings.

Sometimes,
he simply stayed still,
waiting for the brightness to pass.

By the end of the day,
neither had done much.

They returned to the tree,
looked at each other,
and said nothing.

The next day,
everything went back to
the way it was.

The squirrel in the light.
The owl in the dark.

They still crossed paths—

but they stopped trying
to change each other.

The Farmers in the Snow

Two farmers walked
the same road
one winter.

Each had once
picked up a frozen snake

to save its life

and been bitten.

And each had taken

a long time to recover.

One day,

the first farmer

came along that road again.

He saw

another snake in the snow,

stiff from the cold.

He paused.

Then

he crushed it under his boot

and kept walking.

Further ahead,
he spotted
a rabbit trembling in the snow.

He looked at it—
then walked on.

"They are no different,"
he said.

Later,
the second farmer
came down the road.

He saw the snake
but did not go near it.

Then,
he saw the shivering rabbit.

He stopped.

He took some food from his bag,
covered it with his scarf,
and then continued his way.

The snow kept falling.

The road remained unchanged.

About the Author

Erin Yun writes quiet, reflective pieces, often about giving, habits, and relationships.

cloudpress.site

Made in the USA
Coppell, TX
05 June 2026

78999823R00049